Twinkle Dives In

Come flutter by

Butterfly Meadow!

❀

and coming soon . . .

Butterfly Meadow

Twinkle Dives In

by Olivia Moss
illustrated by Helen Turner

SCHOLASTIC INC.

New York Toronto London Auckland Sydney
Mexico City New Delhi Hong Kong Buenos Aires

To Remy Smet, the prettiest butterfly
in the meadow

With special thanks to Narinder Dhami

No part of this publication may be reproduced, stored in a
retrieval system, or transmitted in any form or by any
means, electronic, mechanical, photocopying, recording, or otherwise,
without written permission of the publisher. For information
regarding permission, write to Working Partners Limited, Stanley
House, St. Chad's Place, London, WC1X 9HH, United Kingdom.

ISBN-13: 978-0-545-05457-7
ISBN-10: 0-545-05457-5

Text copyright © 2008 by Working Partners Limited.
Illustrations copyright © 2008 by Scholastic Inc.

All rights reserved. Published by Scholastic Inc., 557 Broadway,
New York, NY 10012, by arrangement with Working Partners Limited.
Series created by Working Partners Limited, London.

SCHOLASTIC, LITTLE APPLE, and associated logos are
trademarks and/or registered trademarks of Scholastic Inc.

12 11 10 9 8 7 6 5 4 3 2 1   8 9 10 11 12 13/0

Printed in the U.S.A.

First printing, June 2008

Contents

CHAPTER ONE

Twinkle

It was a perfect summer morning in Butterfly Meadow. The deep-blue sky overhead was filled with sunshine. Hundreds of colorful butterflies perched on wildflowers, slowly batting their wings back and forth. Others wove their way lazily between the tall blades of grass.

Dazzle unfurled her yellow wings and stretched. She'd slept for a long time, tucked away under a large leaf next to her new friend, Skipper.

"Good morning, Dazzle," said a voice above her. "Did you sleep well?"

Dazzle slid out from under the leaf and saw Skipper perched nearby, spreading her pale blue wings in the sunshine.

"Yes, thank you, Skipper," Dazzle called, fluttering over to join her friend. "Wow, it's awfully hot out today!"

"And it's going to get hotter!" Skipper added. She glanced at the sun as it rose higher in the sky. "Let's cool off in the dawn dew before it disappears."

Skipper launched herself off the leaf, and Dazzle followed. The wildflowers and the grass were still covered with cool droplets of dew, sparkling like crystals in the sunlight. The two butterflies skimmed over them, brushing the petals and leaves with their wings.

"Oh, that's nice!" Dazzle said with a sigh, as the dewdrops cooled her down.

"Be careful not to get your wings too wet," Skipper warned her. "Or you won't be able to fly."

The two butterflies rested for a moment on a large, bobbing thistle. Suddenly, Dazzle noticed a beautiful butterfly whizzing across the meadow. All of the butterflies turned to stare as it landed gracefully on a yellow daisy and waved its wings in greeting. It was much bigger than either Skipper or Dazzle.

Its wings were deep red, with large circles of blue, pale yellow, and dark brown.

"Who's *that*?" Dazzle asked, watching as the big butterfly zigzagged across the meadow, showing off its beautiful wings.

"Oh, it's Twinkle!" Skipper exclaimed as the butterfly fluttered closer.

Dazzle watched as Twinkle landed gracefully on a purple foxglove flower nearby.

"Hello, you must be Dazzle!" Twinkle called out. "I'm Twinkle and I'm a peacock butterfly!" Before Dazzle had a chance to reply, Twinkle began to twirl

slowly on top of the flower. "Look at my wings," she went on. "Have you noticed how they catch the sunlight?"

Skipper glanced at Dazzle. "Twinkle is very proud of her wings, and she likes everyone to know it," she whispered. "It's usually easiest to agree with her!"

"Oh, but I *do* think Twinkle is beautiful," said Dazzle, not bothering to whisper. "I think she's one of the prettiest butterflies I've ever seen."

Twinkle looked pleased. "Thanks, Dazzle! You're not so bad yourself," she said, doing another twirl. "Isn't it hot today? I know the *perfect* place to go on a summer's day like this."

"Where?" Dazzle and Skipper asked together.

"Cowslip Pond!" Twinkle replied.

CHAPTER TWO

To the Pond!

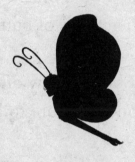

"What's Cowslip Pond?" asked Dazzle.

"It's a beautiful place," Twinkle told her, "especially when the sun is shining. It's not far from here! We can cool off in the water, and the ducks are a lot of fun to be around."

Dazzle narrowed her eyes, confused. "What's a duck?" she asked.

Twinkle zoomed up into the air. "There's only one way for you to find out," she cried, hovering above Dazzle and Skipper. "Follow me to Cowslip Pond!" Twinkle darted off, weaving her way through the clouds of butterflies in the meadow.

Dazzle and Skipper flew after her. A trip to the pond was sure to be an adventure!

"Be careful, you three," called Spot, one of the older butterflies. She was sunning herself on a crimson poppy. "Don't go too far from the meadow."

Dazzle and Skipper didn't even have time to reply. They were too busy trying to keep up with Twinkle, who was zipping along excitedly ahead of them.

"Come on, you two!" Twinkle called. "I can't wait to cool off at Cowslip Pond."

Dazzle and Skipper followed Twinkle across the fields. It seemed like they were flying for a long time. Dazzle was beginning to feel tired when they entered a peaceful little valley. The grass was starred with yellow, pink, and cream flowers. A bird sat in a nearby tree, singing with a *tut-tut-tut* sound.

"That's a thrush," Skipper explained to Dazzle. "And this is Cowslip Valley! See those yellow flowers? They're called cowslips. And there's Cowslip Pond at the other end of the valley." Skipper pointed up ahead.

Dazzle gazed into the distance and could see the cool blue shimmer of water.

"Hurry up!" Twinkle called. She hovered in midair, waiting for Skipper and Dazzle to catch up. "I can't wait to show you the pond."

As Dazzle and Skipper flew over to join her, Dazzle heard a strange clicking noise below them.

"What's that?" she exclaimed, coming to a stop and glancing around in alarm.

"Look down there, Dazzle," Skipper told her. "Next to that patch of pink primroses. Can you see it?"

"See what?" Dazzle asked. She couldn't see *anything*!

A green insect jumped quickly out of the clump of primroses. It landed on a large blade of grass, waving its antennae.

"That's a cricket," Twinkle explained. "It makes that clicking noise you heard by rubbing its wings together."

"Really?" said Dazzle, looking down at the long-legged insect. The cricket glanced up and noticed the three butterflies hovering above.

"Good morning, ladies," it called cheerfully.

"Good morning," Dazzle replied with a friendly wave.

"Come with me!" Twinkle laughed. "I have something else to show you." She led Dazzle across the valley, closer to the pond, while Skipper followed behind. "See those

14

yellow flowers down there, Dazzle?"

"You mean the cowslips?" Dazzle asked.

"No, no!" Twinkle replied. "Cowslips are pale yellow. I'm talking about those smaller golden-yellow flowers. They're called buttercups."

"Buttercups," Dazzle repeated, noticing how the golden petals glowed in the bright sunshine.

"Try flying underneath them, Dazzle," Twinkle told her. "Go on!"

Dazzle dipped down and flew carefully between the clumps of buttercups.

Suddenly, she was bathed in a beautiful golden glow from the shiny petals. Dazzle cried out with delight.

"See?" Twinkle called. "I can show you lots of fun things like that, Dazzle!"

"Oh, Twinkle!" Dazzle said, flying up to meet her two friends again. "Thank you so —"

"Ooh, wow," Twinkle interrupted. "I can see a sunflower! I *must* go sit on it for a minute. It's so tall that everyone will be able to see how *gorgeous* my wings look next to its petals!"

Twinkle fluttered off toward the sunflower without a backward glance.

Dazzle watched her leave, feeling sad. Didn't Twinkle care what she had to say?

CHAPTER THREE

Pond Pals

Dazzle hung her head. She was grateful to Twinkle for bringing her to Cowslip Pond and showing her so many new things along the way. But she was also disappointed that her new friend didn't seem to have time to stop and listen to her!

"Don't feel hurt, Dazzle," Skipper said gently as they flew on toward the pond.

"Twinkle can't help herself. She likes to be the center of attention, and sometimes she forgets that she might hurt people's feelings."

"I just wanted to say thank you," Dazzle said with a sigh, watching Twinkle settle on the large, upturned face of the sunflower. The peacock butterfly's deep red wings sparkled and shimmered against the yellow petals.

"Come on," said Skipper cheerfully. "I can't wait to cool off at the pond. Twinkle won't sit still for long. I'm sure she'll be right behind us!"

Dazzle cheered up as they flew closer to Cowslip Pond. The pond was large, round, and edged with thick clumps of reeds. The green-blue water was dotted with lily pads. It looked cool and inviting! Dazzle couldn't wait to get closer and feel the breeze that rippled across the surface of the water.

"Well, what do you think?" Skipper asked as she and Dazzle hovered above the reeds.

"I think it's amazing —" Dazzle began.

Quack! Quack!

"Oh!" Dazzle gasped and looked around to see what was making the loud noise. She spotted a fluffy little white bird with a yellow beak. It stood on the bank of the pond. "What's *that*, Skipper?"

"That's a young duck," Skipper explained. "There are lots of ducks living here at Cowslip Pond. They're friendly!"

As Dazzle and Skipper watched, Twinkle came swooping toward the pond.

"Hello, Feathers!" she called to the duck. She landed on his beak and gave him a butterfly kiss, fluttering her wings

against his brow. "Dazzle, this is my friend Feathers."

"Pleased to meet you, Feathers," Dazzle called shyly as Twinkle danced off again. She could see now that Skipper was right. Twinkle really *did* care. She just got distracted easily!

"Don't you think I'm beautiful, Feathers?" Twinkle called as she flew over the surface of the pond.

Quack! Feathers agreed. Dazzle and Skipper glanced at each other, and Dazzle felt laughter tickling inside her. Skipper looked like she wanted to giggle, too.

"Watch me air-dive, Dazzle!" Twinkle said, dipping down near the pond. She skimmed across the surface, her wings so

close to the water that it took Dazzle's breath away. "Wheee!"

"Be careful, Twinkle," Skipper called.

"It's so cool down here," Twinkle sighed happily. "And I can see my reflection in the water, too! Come see!"

Dazzle and Skipper skimmed across the pond behind Twinkle. Dazzle loved

the feel of the cool breeze below her
wings, but she didn't dare get as close
to the water as Twinkle did.

"Twinkle's brave, isn't she?" Dazzle
asked Skipper as they flew together.

"Maybe," Skipper replied. "But we're
much safer up here."

As Dazzle fanned her wings slowly in

the breeze, she noticed some brown insects on the surface of the pond. They didn't fly like Dazzle, Twinkle, and Skipper. Instead, they moved quickly across the water on their long, thin legs. Dazzle stared at them in amazement.

"Skipper," she gasped. "What are *those*? I've never seen such long legs."

The insects heard Dazzle and looked up at her.

"We're water striders," one of them called. "We live on the surface of the pond and wait for bugs to fall into the water."

"Why?" Dazzle asked.

"To eat them," the water strider replied matter-of-factly.

"I see," said Dazzle. But she didn't understand. She turned to Skipper, frowning. "Would they really eat another bug?" she whispered.

"Yes," Skipper replied. "We sip nectar. Water striders eat bugs. We all have to eat."

Dazzle flew higher into the air, away from the surface of the

pond. She didn't want to be anybody's lunch!

"Look at me!" Twinkle called just then. She fluttered across the water again. "I'm going to do a really low dive this time! Watch out — here I come!"

CHAPTER FOUR

Twinkle in Trouble

"Oh, no!" Dazzle gasped as Twinkle skimmed across the pond. Her wings almost touched the surface. It looked awfully dangerous. "Skipper, she's too close to the water!"

Just then, Twinkle tried to do one of her spectacular twirls. But she was flying so low that one of her wings skimmed the

surface of the pond. Twinkle tipped to
one side, then the other. She struggled
to steady her wings. With a cry, she
crashed into the water.

"Twinkle!" Dazzle called. She could
see that her friend's wings were
completely wet now. They drooped and
sagged in the water. "Skipper, we have
to help her!"

"Wait, Dazzle," Skipper rushed after her. "We can't get our wings wet, too — that would be a disaster. Then we'd be no help at all to Twinkle!"

Dazzle and Skipper watched helplessly as Twinkle managed to grab on to the edge of a fat green lily pad floating nearby. She dragged herself out of the water and lay there, panting from the effort.

Dazzle and Skipper flew over to the lily pad and hovered above their friend.

"Are you all right, Twinkle?" Dazzle asked urgently. "Are your wings hurt?"

"I don't think so," Twinkle called back weakly. She was gasping for breath and she wouldn't look at her friends. "But they're soaked."

Dazzle glanced down at Twinkle's

33

wings. They hung limply by her sides, dripping water.

"So you can't fly up to us?" Skipper asked, looking worried.

"No, I can't fly at all." Twinkle struggled to lift her wings. "I'm too wet. Oh, I'm a mess! I'll have to wait until I dry out a little."

Dazzle and Skipper circled the lily pad, watching as Twinkle spread her wings in the sunshine. They were so wet and crumpled!

"I wish there was some way to get Twinkle out of the pond," Dazzle said. "Maybe Feathers the duck could help?"

She and Skipper looked around the pond hopefully. "Feathers? Feathers!" they shouted, but Feathers was nowhere to be seen.

"Well, at least the sun is nice and hot," Skipper said with a sigh. "That means Twinkle's wings will dry out quickly."

Just then, Dazzle noticed something moving on the other side of the pond. She glanced over and saw the water striders staring at Twinkle.

"But maybe not fast enough," Dazzle whispered.

Skipper looked puzzled. "What do you mean?" she asked.

"Look over there," Dazzle replied, her heart beating faster.

Now the water striders were skimming across the water. They were headed straight for Twinkle!

CHAPTER FIVE

Looking for Help

"Help!" Twinkle cried, as soon as she saw the insects skating in her direction.

"Oh, Skipper!" Dazzle gasped, frightened. "What are we going to do?"

"We have to try and scare the water striders away from Twinkle," Skipper replied in a determined voice. "Come on, Dazzle!"

Bravely, Skipper and Dazzle swooped straight toward the water striders. As they did, Twinkle tried to move her wings, but they were still soaked through. She couldn't lift them, no matter how hard she tried.

"Hold it right there!" Skipper called loudly, hovering just out of the water

striders' reach. "You shouldn't be coming *this* way."

"Why not?" asked the water strider at the front of the group.

"Because there's a nice fat insect for you over on the other side of the pond, by that big clump of reeds," Dazzle said, pointing. She didn't like telling lies, but they had to help Twinkle. "Why don't you go and see?"

The water striders turned and skimmed eagerly back across the water.

"Now what, Dazzle?" Skipper asked. "We don't have much time before the water striders realize that we tricked them."

Dazzle thought for a moment, fluttering silently in the air.

"Maybe we could fly back to the meadow and get some of the older butterflies," she suggested. "Spot or one of the others may be able to help us."

But Twinkle looked even more frightened when she heard Dazzle's suggestion.

"Oh, *please* don't leave me!" Twinkle cried. "I'm not brave. I don't want to be trapped here, all alone."

"Don't worry, Twinkle," Dazzle said quickly. "We won't leave you."

"There aren't any insects here," one of the water striders shouted from the other side of the pond. "We've been tricked!" He and the others skimmed back across the water, heading straight for Twinkle again.

"We have to call for help," said Skipper. "Someone in the meadow might hear us."

"Good idea," Dazzle agreed. She and Skipper fluttered side-by-side, hovering just above Twinkle. "OK, one, two, three — HELP!"

Skipper and Dazzle called out together
as loudly as they could, but their voices
didn't carry very far.

"We're a long way from the meadow,"
Skipper pointed out, frowning. "I don't
think anyone can hear us."

Dazzle glanced quickly around
Cowslip Pond, looking for anyone who

might be able to help them. But she couldn't see a single butterfly's wing! Twinkle was still stranded in the middle of the pond, and the water striders were getting closer and closer. Dazzle had to think of something quick!

CHAPTER SIX

Dazzle's Great Idea

The water striders skimmed quickly toward Twinkle. They were only a few feet from the lily pad now!

"Look, Dazzle!" Skipper cried in dismay, turning her face to the sky. "The sun has disappeared behind that big cloud. Now Twinkle's wings are going to take even longer to dry."

That was it! Dazzle had an idea. If they could do something to help Twinkle's wings dry, she would be able to fly away from the water striders. . . .

Dazzle remembered how she'd been chased by a blackbird the day before. She had been scared, just like Twinkle, but Skipper had come to her rescue. Dazzle had flown close behind Skipper

as they darted to safety. Even in all the
excitement, the breeze from Skipper's
beating wings had been comforting.

"I know!" Dazzle said suddenly.
"Skipper, we can use our wings to make
a breeze. It will help Twinkle's wings dry
more quickly."

"Dazzle, that's a great idea!" Skipper
gasped excitedly. "Let's go!"

Dazzle and Skipper dipped down near
the lily pad again. Twinkle was huddled
in the center of it, trying to make herself
as small as possible. The water striders
had spread out and were circling the lily
pad. They looked hungry.

"Twinkle, don't panic," Skipper
called. "Just stay still!"

"I don't have any choice," Twinkle
called back helplessly. "My wings are still

too wet to fly!" She raised one wing, but it flopped down again.

"Skipper and I are going to dry them off," Dazzle told her.

Dazzle and Skipper fluttered as close to Twinkle as they could. Dazzle hovered over one of Twinkle's wings, and Skipper over the other. Then both butterflies began to beat their own wings as fast as possible.

"Ooh, I can feel the breeze," Twinkle cried, wriggling with delight. "I can feel my wings drying!"

CHAPTER SEVEN

Twinkle's Escape

"Keep going, Skipper," Dazzle panted. Her wings ached, but she didn't stop fluttering them up and down. Neither did Skipper.

The water striders kept circling the lily pad, their gazes fixed on Twinkle. "What are you doing?" one of them asked, glancing up at Dazzle and Skipper.

"You're not going to eat this insect," Skipper called. "She's too pretty to have for lunch!"

"We don't care what she looks like," the water strider replied. "We're hungry."

Dazzle glared at him and beat her wings even faster.

"Keep going," called a beautiful

bright blue insect hovering near the lily pad.

"That's a dragonfly," Skipper told Dazzle, panting.

"Thank you," Dazzle called to the dragonfly. She could see tiny fish peeking out of the water at them, too. The whole pond was watching the butterflies now!

Suddenly, there was a splash at the side of the pond. Dazzle glanced over. Feathers the duck was swimming toward Twinkle!

Quack! he called, flapping his wings angrily at the water striders. The insects skated out of his way but didn't move far from the lily pad.

"Thank you, Feathers!" Twinkle cried.

She looked much happier as she moved her wings back and forth.

"I think Twinkle's enjoying all the attention," Skipper whispered to Dazzle, grinning.

"I'm going to try and fly," Twinkle announced, giving herself a little shake.

At that moment, the sun broke out from behind the cloud.

"Oh, that's better!" Twinkle said with a sigh as the warm sunshine kissed her wings.

Feathers quacked loudly. Dazzle and Skipper looked down. Some of the water striders were climbing onto the lily pad!

"Do you think you can fly now, Twinkle?" Dazzle called.

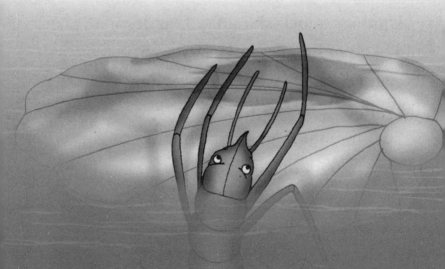

"I can try," Twinkle said, looking frightened.

Slowly, she moved her wings back and forth. Dazzle held her breath as Twinkle fluttered uncertainly upward, then dipped down again. Were Twinkle's wings dry enough to fly?

Determined, Twinkle flapped her wings more strongly. This time she rose up into the air, leaving the lily pad and the water striders behind. Just in time! Dazzle and Skipper bobbed up and down in delight.

"Hooray!" cried Twinkle, doing three twirls in a row. "I'm dry again!"

Feathers, the dragonflies, and the fish watched, their faces shining with happiness. Twinkle celebrated by doing a swift lap of the pond, turning her wings this way and that in the sun.

"Oh, well. You win some, you lose some!" a water strider said. "Let's see what's for lunch on the other side of the pond."

"Go, Twinkle!" Dazzle cheered as Twinkle swooped down to say hello to the little fish bobbing excitedly up and down in the water. "We did it, Skipper!"

CHAPTER EIGHT

Friends for Life

"That's Twinkle for you," Skipper said with a laugh. "Better than ever!"

Dazzle and Skipper flew over to join Twinkle, who was hovering by the edge of the pond.

"Thank you," Twinkle cried, swooping toward them and brushing her beautiful wings against Dazzle's. "It was *your* brilliant idea that helped me escape, Dazzle. If it hadn't been for you and Skipper, I don't know what I would have done!"

"I'm glad you're safe, Twinkle," Dazzle said shyly.

"Me, too," Skipper added.

"I'll never forget what you did for me," Twinkle said. "You two know what this means, don't you?"

Dazzle and Skipper looked at each other, confused.

"It means that we three butterflies are now friends for life!" Twinkle announced.

Dazzle couldn't help grinning. She was proud of herself! Twinkle was a special butterfly, and Dazzle had helped her out of a *very* sticky situation.

"Oh, look down there," Twinkle said, dipping down near the reeds at the edge of the pond. "See the family of ladybugs on that blade of grass?"

Dazzle and Skipper watched as
Twinkle hovered near the ladybugs.

"Hi, ladybugs!" she called. "Look at
the amazing markings on my wings!
Have you ever seen anything so pretty?"

The ladybug family stopped to stare
at Twinkle. Dazzle and Skipper glanced
at each other and laughed.

"Good old Twinkle," said Dazzle.

"She'll never change," Skipper added. "And we love her just the way she is!"

"Those are my two best friends, Dazzle and Skipper," Twinkle told the ladybugs. "They saved my life today. They are the most beautiful butterflies in all of Butterfly Meadow!"

Dazzle couldn't believe her ears. Twinkle zoomed over to Dazzle and Skipper.

"Do you mean that?" asked Dazzle as Twinkle landed on a flower beside her. The beautiful butterfly nodded as the flower bobbed up and down.

"Absolutely," Twinkle said. "It's not all about how you look. It's what you do that counts."

Dazzle had never had anyone tell her that she was beautiful before!

"It's true," said Skipper as she landed on a third flower. "You were wonderful today, Dazzle." Feathers the duck swam by and gave a loud quack of agreement.

Dazzle was so full of happiness that she couldn't stay on the flower a moment longer. She flew up into the air and traced pretty patterns in the blue sky as she fluttered over Twinkle and Skipper.

"Come on!" she called out to her friends. The other two butterflies batted their wings and rose up into the air beside her. Together, the three friends flew through the sunshine back to Butterfly Meadow.

✖ FUN FACTS! ✖
Life as a Butterfly

How would you like to taste with your feet? Breathe through your side? Have a straw for a tongue and antennae for a nose? If you were a butterfly, that is exactly how you'd live!

TASTE

Butterflies taste with their feet. They must stand on something with their six legs to find out if it is good enough to eat! Butterflies have a tongue that is like a long straw. They use it to drink nectar.

SMELL

Butterflies don't use noses to breathe or smell. They breathe through small openings on the sides of their bodies, and smell through the antennae on the tops of their heads!

SIGHT

Butterflies have eyes, but they can see all the way around their bodies — without turning their heads! Part of their eyes also acts like a magnifying glass, so they can see things up close.

HEARING

If you thought the butterflies' wings were only for flying, think again! Not only are butterfly wings beautiful, but they also help butterflies hear. Their wings can sense changes in sound vibrations.

Now you will never look at a butterfly the same way again!

Dazzle is finally at home in

Butterfly Meadow!

Here's a sneak peek at her next
adventure,

Three Cheers for Mallow!

CHAPTER ONE

Talent Search

". . . Eight, nine, ten! Ready or not,
here I come!" called Dazzle. She was
playing hide and seek with her best friend
Skipper, in Butterfly Meadow. Dazzle
looked around, hoping to spot a flash of
Skipper's blue wings. There was no sign
of her. Where was Skipper hiding?

Dazzle fluttered through the air,
searching the tall feathery grasses and

colorful flowers. Ah! There was a splash of blue in the long grass. Was it Skipper?

She dipped low for a closer look. No, it was a clump of bright cornflowers! Their blue heads were turned to the sun as they swayed in the gentle breeze.

Dazzle flew toward a patch of tall violet flowers. Maybe Skipper was hiding there. "I'm coming to find you!" she sang out, hoping her friend would giggle in reply.

Instead, a different butterfly's voice called out behind her. "All right, Team Butterfly! Let's G-O, go!"

Dazzle turned in surprise as a cloud of colorful butterflies swirled up from some nearby flowers, chattering and laughing. What was all the excitement about?

Skipper darted out from where she'd been hiding in the rambling rose. "Come on!" she cried.

"What's going on?" Dazzle asked, confused.

"Today is Sports Day," Skipper explained. "You know Mallow, the white butterfly over there. She's organizing it, just like she organized the party on your first day in Butterfly Meadow!"